Ronald Morgan Goes to Camp

Ronald Morgan Goes to Camp

by Patricia Reilly Giff • illustrated by Susanna Natti

PUFFIN BOOKS

PUFFIN BOOKS
Published by the Penguin Group
Penguin Books USA Inc., 375 Hudson Street, New York, New York 10014, U.S.A.
Penguin Books Ltd, 27 Wrights Lane, London W8 5TZ, England
Penguin Books Australia Ltd, Ringwood, Victoria, Australia
Penguin Books Canada Ltd, 10 Alcorn Avenue, Toronto, Ontario, Canada M4V 3B2
Penguin Books (N.Z.) Ltd, 182-190 Wairau Road, Auckland 10, New Zealand

Penguin Books Ltd, Registered Offices: Harmondsworth, Middlesex, England

First published in the United States of America by Viking,
a division of Penguin Books USA Inc., 1995
Published in Puffin Books, 1997

1 3 5 7 9 10 8 6 4 2

THE LIBRARY OF CONGRESS HAS CATALOGED THE VIKING EDITION AS FOLLOWS:
Giff, Patricia Reilly.
Ronald Morgan goes to camp / by Patricia Reilly Giff;
illustrated by Susanna Natti. p. cm.
Summary: Ronald Morgan is afraid he won't get a medal at camp because he's not especially good
at swimming or running or singing, but on Medal Day he discovers what he is really good at.
ISBN 0-670-86195-2
[1. Camps—Fiction. 2. Friendship—Fiction.]
I. Natti, Susanna, ill. II. Title
PZ7.G3626Rof 1995 [Fic]—dc20 94-43074 CIP AC

Puffin ISBN 0-14-055647-8

Printed in the United States of America

for Erica Bernhardt and Alice Giff,
True Friends
—P. R. G.

to Robert,
the one and only,
My Irrepressible Dad

dad

—S. N.

It was summer.

School was over.

"Bad news," *R.m.* I said. "There's nothing to do."

"Good news, Ronald Morgan," said Michael.

"We can go to camp."

"Good," said Jan.

"Great," said Rosemary. "Maybe we can win some medals."

"Yes," said Michael. "You just have to be good at something."

I thought for a minute.

I wasn't good at anything.

"I don't think I'll go," I said.

But Billy shook his head. "Then you'll really have nothing to do."

Billy was right.
My father brought up my suitcase,
and my mother sewed on name tags.
At the last minute, I filled my pockets
with my old green sunglasses,
the harmonica Aunt Ruth gave me,
two plaid Band-Aids just in case,
a cracker, and a box of raisins
that I found under my socks.

Everyone came to the station, even Lucky. (dog)
My father yelled, "Good-bye!"
My mother threw a kiss.
And Aunt Ruth called, "Don't forget to write."
"Uh oh," I said, "I think I forgot to pack
a pencil."

Inside the bus we sang:
> *Friends we make*
> *at Camp Echo Lake . . .*

But Rosemary didn't sing.
"I'm going to win a pile of medals,"
she was telling the bus driver.
"For swimming, and diving,
and running, and . . ."
I didn't sing either.
I was trying to think of something
I was good at.

R.M

And Jan didn't sing.

"I always get sick on the bus," she said.

R.m
I reached into my pocket.

I gave her some raisins.

"Try these," I said. "Maybe you'll feel better."

"They have dust on them," she said.

"But they're really good."

Then Jimmy yelled, "Hey! We're here!
It's Camp Echo Lake."
Ms. Conrad, our counselor, was waiting.
"Call me Connie," she said.
She walked us back and forth to see
the lake, the hill, and the pine trees.

"Look," said Michael.

R.m & michael

We slid down to watch a green frog,

and then a duck with a bunch of brown

feathers, who was quacking at us.

"What a great swimmer," Michael said.

R.m

I broke up a cracker for the duck.

"Do you think I'm good at anything?" I asked.
Michael raised his shoulders in the air.
"Sure," he said. "I guess so."
We quacked as we ran to catch up
with everyone.
Tom was saying,
"I think that's a poisonous bug."
I looked closer.
"I think it's only a daddy-long-legs."

On Tuesday, we had bug juice
and bananas for a snack.
Jan had another raisin, too.
Then I sat up on Lookout Rock
and practiced my song.
In out, in out . . . on the harmonica.

12

It *almost* sounded like
    Friends we make
    at Camp Echo Lake . . .
"Look out, rock!" Michael yelled.
"I'm climbing up."
But he slipped.
I dived to catch him, and we rolled
down the hill together.
It was kind of fun.

And then it was time to swim.

Maybe I was good at that.

Connie called out, "Ready . . . set . . . jump!"

Rosemary was the first one in.

"Look," she said. "A little snake."

And I said, "I think I'll call him Snakey."

But Tom yelled, "That snake is after me!"

I took giant steps across the rocks to pull

him out, but I splashed into the water.

"Quack," said Michael.

"Quack," I said back.

On Wednesday, Connie said,
"It's time for hide-and-seek."
Billy counted: "Two four six . . ."
Michael ran one way, Jan ran the other.
"Raisins make me go fast," she called back.

Tom and I crashed through the bushes.
"Hey," Tom said,
"we're lost in a mosquito nest."
I played my harmonica as loud as I could,
so someone could find us.
"You're IT, Ronald Morgan," Billy said.
But first I pulled out the Band-Aids
to cover the bites.
One for Tom and one for me.

17

Thursday night was camp-out.

I wore my sweats with the muddy knees.

At the campfire, we toasted

marshmallows on sticks.

We told stories, too.

Michael told about a dog,

and Alice told about a ghost,

a GREAT GRAY SCARY—

"Stop!" said Jan, with her hands over her ears.

I'm not so good at stories,

so instead I played my harmonica,

and everyone sang:

> *Friends we make*
> *at Camp Echo Lake . . .*

On Friday, we made *I Missed You* cards
for our mothers and fathers.
I drew one for Lucky, too.
"Nice work," Connie told everyone.

20

But Jimmy said, "I *really* miss my mother.
I miss my TV, too."
"Wait," I said.
I lent him my old green sunglasses
so no one would know his eyes were red.

And then it was Saturday.

Medal Day.

First we drew pictures.

Then we stuck tiny stones on the paper
with glue.

"Work hard," said Connie.

"We'll show them to everyone."

We spent a long time looking for stones.

Then we rushed to clean and pack

and make lemonade, because

people were coming up the drive.

My mother and father, Aunt Ruth,

and even Lucky in a picnic basket.

"It's medal time," said Connie.

"Everyone was good at something."

I shook my head. "Not me."

Rosemary's medal was for swimming,

and Jan's was for running.

Billy's was for hide-and-seek,

and Michael's was for telling stories.

At last it was my turn.

"Ronald . . ." said Connie.

I held my breath.

"You get a medal for . . .

being a good friend."

"She's right," said Michael.

"Yes," said Jan.

And everybody cheered.

Then I played the harmonica
one last time, while everybody sang:
Friends we make
At Camp Echo Lake . . .